CELESTIAL RUST

Dean Kostos

12/2/95

For Larry + Arnie,

all the best,

Dean

Red Dust • New York

Dedicated to Anna, Sofia and Theodore

I would like to thank the reviews where some of these poems first appeared: *Boulevard*, *The Chiron Review*, *The James White Review*, *National Forum*, *City Rant*, *Exquisite Corpse*, *Colorado North Review*, *Tamarind*, and *New Hesperia*.

Cover: from Odilon Redon's *Winged Man or Fallen Angel*

Celestial Rust by Dean Kostos
copyright © 1994 Dean Kostos

Published by Red Dust, Inc.
All rights reserved

ISBN 0-87376-077-8

Book design by Tomm Scalera

CIRCUIT CURRENT

I dream I pass through God's veins:

Streets swerve like molten pythons;
Windowpanes flash like scales.
When a billion white butterflies thrash in a glass skull,
A paperweight full of snow falls on the city:

Ghosts steam from street gratings,
Clasping parts of their bodies
They considered most important the moment
They died: One covers its mouth, one its crotch,
One holds a red jacket
With its initials embroidered in human hair.

I'm afraid if I stand here too long
The vapors will enter my soles, then into my soul,
The way Greeks believed *daimons* of inspiration
Entered them from the soil,
Flushing through their veins like electricity.

Rushing down the street, I see lamps
Blur an intoxicating light.
And right here—between the Appellate Court
And that church whose sayings change weekly—
I enter some celestial corridor, when

Three men come toward me;
Passing cars shoot their shadows forward.
Weaving into each other, like black flames
Lipped with light, the shadows consume me.
The men chuckle in flickering coats.

Swept down a street, lined with banks,
I see rows of youths with untied shoes, leaning on cars.
Each holds a note under his tongue
Like someone about to commit suicide who can't decide
Whether to gulp the pill.
One youth slants his head like a Brancusi egg
And drills me with his eyes.

I see school windows pasted with paper mummies,
Gilt and glittered by insane children
Who've crayoned hieroglyphs: Dogs, TVs
Full of blood, hands that might be trees or bodies,
And parents' names spelled backward like spells.

When I get where I am going,
I forget where I was going.
When I forget where I am going,
I get where I was going, and find myself
Looking through an enormous window
The way parents do at newborns. Inside:

The central Con Edison office.
All the lights are out.
Women write letters at dark desks
Beside a display dedicated to spring:
On a throne upholstered in feathers,
A three-foot egg nestles.
The round pedestal spins on a motor
Where a generator groans under the ground.

Two men stand on an ocean-colored carpet:
One a gray-bearded black man,
Waving arms as if swimming,
While he explains something
To a younger white man in a black suit.
A light flares from the man's beard,
Its glow invading my chest.

And I think things have lost their edges:
That my self doesn't begin and end with my skin,
That I can swim through everything like a warm ocean.
I think I have died

When the egg shatters like a burst of laughter.
A creature uncoils from the shards,
Crawling close till I can see
The infant me.

THE SENTENCE THAT ENDS WITH A COMMA

Sentences ending with commas
became the only kind I could speak,
swirling from the corners of my mouth,
they tangled round lampposts, following
me like leashes of a dog pack, growing longer and longer
till I fled to the library to find some book

of instructions to sever them, but all the books
I found had run-on sentences linked with commas
within stanzas and paragraphs that longed
to end, but, like inky sperm cells issued from speech,
the commas swam through each thought, following
its logic, hoping the mouths

that gave birth to them would mouth
their conclusion, whether in speech or book,
so I went from state to state, following
specialists who lectured on *The Finite Use of the Comma*,
but as I listened, whips hissed from their speech,
wrapping round their feet (they were so long),

the chaos I'd longed
to organize seemed to have taken root in my mouth,
and I realized that even if I didn't speak,
my confusion wouldn't cease, so I decided to book
into an asylum where you're taught to float in a coma,
yet when I saw the zero eyes of the asylum's following

I bolted, having no lead to follow
but fear or intuition, which no longer
curled on top of my head like a cartoon comma,
but hid under the roof of my mouth,
so I razored captions from philosophy books,
gluing them round my tongue to control my speech,

yet my voice asserted its own life each time I'd speak:
soon no one recognized me, for my sentences followed
so often, I resembled a string-ball seen in children's books,
then it became clear one morning: I'd no longer
attempt to remedy my mouth's
ills, instead, would welcome the commas

to seed more commas throughout my speech,
allowing my mouth its own life, following
its hunger, longing for what can't be contained by words or books,

AUBADE: LOOKING BACKWARD
for Sofia

There in the undergrowth,
   The shadow of a glove
      Filled with the night before:

A rain of eyelashes
   Drilled holes through solitude.
      She looked back

To a discarded shell,
   Found a blade and cut a pattern
      In the shape of wings.

While night's needle sang back its black
   Like a scratched 78 r.p.m.,
      She threaded seeds to her eyelids

And entered the halls of sleep:
   In doorway after doorway loomed
      Ghosts of men with hissing radios

Who coiled her waist with arms
   Tattooed with snakes and hearts.
      As the sweat of chrysanthemums

Lines the glove, she wakes
   In the shell of a damaged music,
      Wipes the voices from her eyes,

Cracks open the door,
   And, stepping in,
      Wraps herself in a rain of shadows.

DREAM: AN UNKNOWING

I dream-wake from dreaming :
Night's wind-fist bursts through curtains.

An aquarium by the window
Swirls black feather-fish.

Suddenly, my cat pounces on water's skin,
Plunging in with a SLAP!

I sit up, a clump of feathers flies
Into my mouth, caged between teeth.

Like a strip of dipped litmus,
From head down I become a shadow.

Embarrassed, my cat leaps free from the tank,
Arching out on a watery necklace.

Fur bristling like spikes, paws
Bunches of black feathers,

She fights a tangle of wind
As if it were a demonic bird.

Wild-eyed, she slinks under sheets
I've abandoned while

I stand by the window, bathed in streetlight,
Watching it melt my shadow-self.

SHE'S SICK RIGHT NOW, BUT YOU'LL SEE HER AGAIN SOON

As the husks of summer peeled away
a black car curved into our driveway.
Mom eased out of her seat, balancing
a glass smile in her hands.

The Sunday-choir mouths of the people next door
hissed "Crazy Germs!"

When I walked down the hill, neighbors' faces
snarled with fists:
"Crazy boy, just like your mother!
We don't want the crazy-germs
brewing in your boiling eyes!
We don't want you near our houses!"–
Strung with gallstones and Christmas Lights.
–"We don't want you on our lawns!"
Plots not of grass but of claws.

All their doors clamped shut.

I tried to giggle, then to cry out,
feeling on my face the suction
of my teachers' hands like leeches.

Hurtling toward the barricade,
I pried open the bricks and slipped between them
to wear the leprous wall.

My hurt self pleaded: *Please protect me* . . .

But I couldn't answer, for a swarm of neighbors
circled outside, shrinking my voice
with the beaks of their fingers.

Mom knew these people
who strung their hours like necklaces of teeth,
who dipped their watches in acid like teabags.
She heard the wag of their ticking tongues
but was mute before them.

Days home from the asylum,
she held my hand, squeezing it hard
and with her eyes said:
I can't help you; I hate myself for this.

An adult now, I crawl
from that enclosure at the base of the hill
where starched houses arch in succession
like a bite mark.

ELEGY FOR A LIVING MAN
for Theodore,
with Parkinson's disease

While waves thrashed in the distance,
my father's body hardened into a pillar of salt.

Shadow-shafts spoked from the base,
shifted like clock hands, ticking away sun.

Voices crowded his skull with pleas;
his crippled lips couldn't answer.

When feathery shadows erased his dust-scrawled names
(:lawyer, politician, speaker),

darkness consumed his room.
Like a pair of egrets, his moonpolished eyes

fluttered to a replica of our family—
molded by him, preserved in a jar of brine.

Flinching, his eyes returned to socket-
caves, numbed into sleep:

Regrets flocked from nightmare-swamps,
beating wings and beaks against the glass

as though starving, and his body
a mound of dying fish.

A specter of the man he'd hoped to be
slid from his side, passed through the glass

to battle the beasts like Saint George
with a sword that severs past from present.

The assault muted the squawks:
RECALL? RECALL? RECALL? . . .

Sun sliced the horizon. The regrets scattered,
blood splattered on question-mark necks.

A few feathers quivered on the panes.
Dad opened his eyes as I

wrestled him into his wheelchair.
Screeching along the carpet,

the wheels' spokes, like antennas, flashed
with the static of things unspoken.

From his tongue's cocoon, words flitted:
"Uh-yee nayveur woonteed hoort-oort yeeou..."

Cupped in prayerful gesture, his hands filled with
something unseen which he tendered

to friends long dead, his mother, his father.
"Oo-whyy woor they-ee heeyere?"

He swatted the air, besieged
by insects with human heads.

Blued by TV's flicker, he curved into his wheelchair,
eyes dazing:

From his tracheotomy-hole,
an iridescent weave of lightning

rushed up in the form of a dancer, free
to move, to loosen sinew and bone.

The dancer spun, coaxing him: *Let me go.*
When its spinning churned the carpet to sand,

Dad and I sat on the beach again.
I pressed my face to the grainy warmth:

Like a brave listening for hoofbeats, I
heard a heartbeat and plunged in my hands,

wrenching out an infant heart.
I rescued it from a strangle of roots,

secured the pounding bulb with toothpicks
above a jar of tears,

and placed it on a ledge near the ocean
which sputtered his name, his *nay me:*

The ore adored
He the ardor   the odor   the O-door

Theodore

INTENDING TO SPEAK
Sitges, Spain

Intending to speak in past tense,
I entered your house, calling your name.
A Spanish opera floated from the stereo,
But no one was home.

Calling your name, I entered each room:
All the beds were unmade,
But not one was warm.
Dogs yelped from salt-colored hills,

Crumpled as unmade beds.
As I peeled away husks of things we'd said,
Dogs yelped from salt-colored hills,
Geraniums unfisted their carmine.

As I peeled away husks of things we'd said,
I waited below your balcony
Where geraniums unfisted their carmine,
Wreathing me in a blood-drop nest.

As I waited below your balcony,
A Spanish opera floated from the stereo.
Wreathed in its blood-drop nest,
I decided to speak in present tense.

BELOW MY BALCONY
Seville, Spain

One prostitute sobs in the arms of another:
Their pietà draped over the curb.
Disco's neon bleeds in a puddle
As electric music throbs and pounds.

From the pietà draped over the curb,
The girl continues to wail.
Electric music throbs and pounds
Like the hooves of Flamenco dancers.

The girl continues to wail
As boys growl, "Putas! Putas!"
With the hooves of Flamenco dancers,
They clatter onto coughing Vespas.

Boys growl, "Putas! Putas!"
Stuffing dark laughs in their pockets,
They scatter away on coughing Vespas,
Erasing whatever happened.

She stuffs dark tears in her pockets
As disco's neon bleeds in a puddle,
Dissolving whatever happened when
This prostitute sobbed in the arms of another.

IN THE JARDIN BOTANICO
Madrid

A bony old man squats down,
  Picking up kumquats
    That scatter from his hands.

Taking shelter from the sun,
  A pride of blue-jeaned youths
    Chatters by the fountain.

Affirming fertility:
  Scents of thyme, pine
    And geranium leaves.

IN HER CHAPEL
La Catedral de Santa Teresa
Avila, Spain

She steps from a grotto of ormolu flames;
Her right hand hovers, blessing, warning.

A torch-like crown sprouts from her scalp;
A honey-fog seethes from her pores

As the chapel breathes,
Breathing out the scent of roses.

Perched on skeletal columns, putti
Whorl clouds from their nostrils.

Bearing Teresa's mortal bones,
A sarcophagous altar sits by her feet.

And the chapel breathes,
Breathing out the scent of roses,

Intoxicating me
Like the spider threading the chandelier.

Tugging her star-sewn mantilla,
Teresa uneclipses her face

And her bird-neck—rising from a nest of frill—
Curves toward me.

Stitched with trumpets formed like mouths
And with scrolls like monkey tails,

Her apron bulges. What does it hold:
A heel of bread, a healing?

The room radiates heat
As if the sun lay buried below the floor,

But I can't move, her mind smelted to mine.
I gulp for air when

Into my lungs the chapel breathes,
Breathing out the scent of roses.

And she gathers this essence to her breasts,
Cradling its invisible bouquet:

Infant version of herself
She again and again gives birth to.

Ormolu: alloys used to resemble gold.

SEEKING SHADE
Segovia, Spain

A Gothic church lunges before me.

A gaggle of teens at its entrance:
Boys on Vespas, girls giggling, their hands
fluttering like birds through dark hair.

Shadow-fingers flicker me inside.
From the vestibule wall, Jesus
looms like a leprous scarecrow:
His knees peeled away like parchment, each bleeding
in the shape of a beard.
His feet clench a bar of wood where he dances
his weight in contrapposto.
From a huge clove that pierces each foot,
spiders of blood explode.

And I want to rescue this man, this God
I've never seen so broken.

The Mass begins before the priest's garden of flames.
Rows of white-haired señoras repeat after him:
"Mea culpa, mea culpa, mea maxima culpa . . ."

My eyes fix on the lance wound.
Gaping like a pummeled mouth, it seems to whimper:
I am your suffering, the voice you never answer.
Its blood-drool scrawls along his ribs.

His glass eyes glare through a web of tears
as if insects were gnawing his guts.
Brown blood curls down his brow like bangs,
and a dusty wig of human hair hangs
from his head like a scalp from a spear.

Out through the doors:
The girls still flirting, hair
still flitting in their hands.

And the hands of the crucifix
clasp like claws, to grasp something
or tender it to me:
Drink, for I am a cup, split and spilt . . .

ICON

Impaled through its eye, the record
Wailed: "C'mon Kyrie,
Light my eleison . . .
When you're strange . . .
O Christos, O baby, hallelujah!"

Jim Morrison's flag of hair
Blew across my eyes as he
Peeled off his shirt.
The groin-guitar groaned:
"Baby, baby, light my. . ."

On my knees.
Cheesecloth swagged Jesus' loin
Just enough to wring a sigh.
Biceps and pectorals grinned
While he draped across the cross

As if it were elegant furniture.
I bowed down, "But Lord,
I fondle myself as I think of You,
Then Jim, then You.
Forgive my dust."

The record spun. Kyrie eleison.
(You spun the web faster, Christos.)
I lay under my milky blanket,
Stuck to my desire.
Nail through the eye of a spider.

TERRAIN: 2 AM

The legs of hanged people dangle from my ceiling
Like roots tangling into a cave.
They're different lovers I once had.

Their callused soles, etched like parchment maps,
Had endlessly led to flesh destinations
Which, when met, shriveled like rinds.

I lie awake in the bed of a ghost river. Once
Spilled with silt and tongued by leaf spears,
Now it gapes, dry

As the mouth of a dying man.
Its clay crazes into pictograms, spelling:
If only again and again

Along the scrawl of vanished currents.
As siroccos howl over the shards,
Sand hisses through sockets, jawbones:

"Alone," "O," "All," "One," "No," "No one," "Ah," "Lone..."
I curl beneath our sheets, part of their topography,
And chart the fissures in the wall,

Bleached, bald as the skull of the man inside me
Who once believed
Each of these lovers was love.

EROS SLEEPING
after an Hellenistic sculpture

You may think my voice has changed
to a flute's voice filtered by Dream,
soft as this stone I make my pillow,

but this bronze you see is a reproduction
of that moment
when my arrow hissed inside you.
Releasing my fingers from day's labor,
I curled inside this metal
as though it were a shell.

You say I'm sleeping,
but I never sleep,
for in your dreams I speak the loudest.
Are you not dreaming now?

The cloth of my chiton floats below me
in dark currents recalling Lethe.
You refer to Death as "sleep"

and I sail there on this stone bed,
as though a boat,
as though a coffin,
parting mists on onyx waters:

Layer past layer, I pass and enter
as breath enters me, huge and rushing,
inflating, deflating my belly
and groin:

I am the flute that lures you.

CELESTIAL RUST

The animal curves the shell, not the shell the animal,
But instead of the living,
Back there comes to every house, ash from the flame,
Ash wet with tears, ash filling urns.
Lined up in rows, they wait
To return to the families that gave them birth.

Between the planks of nature
And the architecture as written, I built a village
Like one in a dream,
Gluing textures into slabs, carving façades.
A movie-glow exalted my art: a stage
Sprouting cardboard arcades. Following the skein
Of canals, gardens, trash dumps, I
Added people, subtracted fur;
Positioned the Colosseum, the temple,
The disco, the prison, the slum.

One Sunday afternoon, below a bridge,
I was surrounded by a swarm of heads and arms
Swiveling round an axis I couldn't see.
In the street piled with error's debris
Where broken machines wheeze a language,
Where plague crawls and cankers—
I had no voice to cry out with.

A yowl rose from the vaults:
"I've lost my hunger! I'm wasting away!"
His teeth darkened against transparent lips,
The fade-to-black working like a curtain . . .

A voice in the crowd spoke of animals' place in nature:
"Nothing sacred to their hooves and nibbling snouts.
They came and roamed and sucked at one another.
Many of us called them 'absences':

Their heads were woozily formed, brows
hanging over eyesockets. Some peered from floppy hats,
Some had faces without faces. Believing they were free,
The beasts thrashed into the sky
Where barbed wire nets glittered."

In his fever, the wasting man heard a whisper:
"There are days when day is discarded.
Animals bray without being answered.
Nameless is the source of creation,
Yet things have a Mother and She has a name:
Mater-matter, mater-matter . . ."

I made small sketches almost against my will:
Columns, girders, domes. Brittle as a mummy's skin,
The pages crumbled in my hands.

Now the wasting man wears a gown
Made of thirty pounds of his flesh, and waits
By the Centers for Disease Control,
Straining for breath when night enfolds him.
I carve a path through his shadows.

The Woman appears.
When hills dissolve into plains, Her temple
Can be seen in the background:
"Whatever country my words evoke around you
Will outlive the landscape you create.
Adjust your eyes to a pinpoint scale,
For holes too wide will sear the retina:
Watching friends and lovers die."

Along the horizon, a wound widened like an eye.
I considered building a dome above it—a lens
To look at heaven—but remembered one the Romans cast.
Their complete collapse smashed the glass
And the act of seeing. Some witnesses yelped
With alarm; some repeated theories.

We wrote our names on papers
And parts of bark until
Lesions gnawed them away.
A flurry of our paper scraps scatters across the plains

Where the Woman turns earth's gears
Loose: celestial wheels
Roll from land to land, house to house,
Past fallen empires, edicts on posts,
Skin shriveling from bones.

"Open your windows and come through them;
Live with river and beasts. Behold, I make all things few."
Now She smooths the waters and speaks Her name,
But we animals
—Curving back into shells—can't hear.

By crumbling façades, recalling frescoed landscapes,
I watch our layered shades
Melt and bleed down the stage
To a faceless harvest, the sun's last blood,
Voices washing behind the horizon.

And above us all, celestial rust.